STAY!

Alex Latimer

PICTURE CORGI

STAY!
A PICTURE CORGI BOOK 978 0 552 56940 8
Published in Great Britain by Picture Corgi, an imprint of Random House Children's Publishers UK
A Penguin Random House Company

Penguin
Random House
UK

This edition published 2015
1 3 5 7 9 10 8 6 4 2
Copyright © Alex Latimer, 2015
The right of Alex Latimer to be identified as the author and illustrator of this work has been asserted
in accordance with the Copyright, Designs and Patents Act 1988.
All rights reserved. No part of this publication may be reproduced, stored in a retrieval system, or transmitted in any form or
by any means, electronic, mechanical, photocopying, recording or otherwise, without the prior permission of the publishers.

Picture Corgi Books are published by Random House Children's Publishers UK,
61–63 Uxbridge Road, London W5 5SA

www.randomhousechildrens.co.uk www.randomhouse.co.uk

Addresses for companies within The Random House Group Limited can be found at: www.randomhouse.co.uk/offices.htm
THE RANDOM HOUSE GROUP Limited Reg. No954009
A CIP catalogue record for this book is available from the British Library.
Printed in China

MIX
Paper from
responsible sources
FSC® C018179

The Random House Group Limited supports the Forest Stewardship Council (FSC®), the leading international
forest-certification organisation. Our books carrying the FSC label are printed on FSC®-certified paper. FSC is the
only forest certification scheme supported by the leading environmental organisations, including Greenpeace.
Our paper procurement policy can be found at www.randomhouse.co.uk/environment

Ben thought his dog Buster was
the best dog in the whole world . . .

But Mum and Dad were not so sure . . .

BUSTER!

"Holiday!"

Ben was over the moon.

Until he remembered
the last holiday . . .

Don't let Buster off the lead if you see any of the following...

In fact, the more Ben thought about it,
the more notes there were to write . . .

'A few things for Buster'

Dad's slipper, so he doesn't chew yours.

My teddy.

Dog biscuits (2 if he's been good, only 1 if he's been bad.)

His lead for walkies.

Food bowl. Stand back wh. he eats – it ac...

...those Buster's paw prints?

No – neighbour's cat.

Yes, that's him.

No – dad.

No – a bird.

...ten t...

...Sc...

When should Buster have a bath?

② When he's changed colour. (unless he's green – then straight to the vet.)

☐ good
☑ OK
☐ bad

① Your eyes sting when you pat him.

④ When he's had a long day.

③ Before Aunt Agnes visits.

...urite Season

...umn is
for squi...

Twi...

How many time...

bark

Ten

One bark is ok

bark bark bark

Best spots for a scratch. in order of preference

② rump   ③ ears   ⑤ snout

① belly

Wh... does Buster need to wee?

...you sit down

In the car

...ht o'c...

How to whistle for Bu...

...dinner time...

You know you're hugging Buster too hard when:

He starts panting

His eyes bulge

crork   He makes a croaking sound

He farts   poot   means...

NOT BaaBaa black sheep. (makes him want to chase sheep.)

...ong

...tch ...atch

to si...

twinkle,

...le diddle.

And by the time the family were ready to set off on their holiday, Ben had more notes than he could count.

"I feel as though I've forgotten something important," Ben said to Grampa.
"Well, if you remember you can always send it to me on a postcard," replied Grampa. "Now have a great time!"

Ben hugged Buster goodbye (careful not to squeeze too tightly!).

Ben did have a great time on holiday, but he kept remembering things that he'd forgotten to tell Grampa.
So he wrote them all down
on postcards . . .

barking at in the middle of the night?

funny noises

nothing

Things Buster shouldn't eat:

Post Card

For Correspondence   Address Only

egg shells

sweet wrappers

chocolate

compost

furniture

peanut butter from the jar

What's Buster dreaming of?

chasing squirrels (don't wake him, he'll be sad.)

tongue out means he's dreaming about dinner

Where does Buster

water bowl

Toilet

fish pond

But there was still something important he was sure he'd forgotten . . .

When Mum started to feel sick after eating a bad hotdog, it reminded Ben of something to tell Grampa.

Diagnosis Chart
(what's wrong with Buster?)

sunburn

love sick

x-ray

ate a toy dinosaur

just needs a wee

And when Dad took the wrong turn on the way to see a famous waterfall, Ben wrote another note.

If Buster gets lost, where will he be?

POSTALE.   POSTKARTE.

(FOR ADDRESS ONLY.)

waiting outside school

sleeping under a tree

tipping over rubbish bins

chasing deer in the park

chasing the postman

But it was only then that he remembered the very important thing he'd forgotten – and he wrote one last note as quickly as he could.

IMPORTANT!

Never take Buster to the post office!

He knows that's where postmen come from.

Love Ben

But the note arrived too late. Grampa and Buster were already on their way to the post office to pick up a parcel.

Buster was banned from the post office! And Grampa thought that perhaps it was time to cure Buster of his bad behaviour.

So he began to train Buster.

... missing you.

Ben couldn't help it – he hugged Grampa
and Buster as hard as he could.

In the weeks that followed, Grampa gave Ben a few extra notes about how to train Buster.

And they worked so well that Mum even suggested Buster come along on the next family holiday.

This time he didn't
bark (or fart) in the car.

And he didn't chase
any birds at all.

He was a very
well-behaved dog . . .

Well, most of the time!

BUSTER!